Welcome To My Weekly Sport Diary, where I Will Dot Down My Wonderful Experience Of Each Week

Name:...

Address:...

....

Sport:...

Team:...

Coach:...

Next of Kin:.................................

Contact Number:.........

D0274354

	What Am Going To Achieved	Thing's Achieved
1		
2		
3		
4		
5		
6		
7		
8		
9		
10		
11		
12		
13		
14		
15		
16		
17		
18		

No one can improve in their game, without understanding the sports techniques

This diary will help me learn from my mistake

So I can plan for my next game

My Pledge

To play and enjoy myself
To maintain my honour
To have faith in Winning
And always strive to Win
Even if I lose!

Date

Weather

The Opponent Team

Match Time

Match Location

Feelings Toward The Match

Highlight Of The Match: ------------------

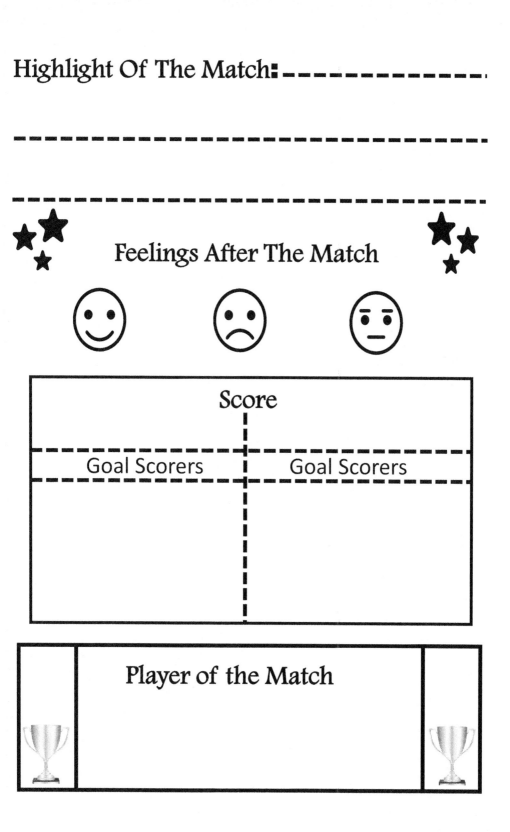

Feelings After The Match

Score

Goal Scorers	Goal Scorers

Player of the Match

Skills To Work On

Tactics for my Next Game

Word of Advice

My Hero of the Week

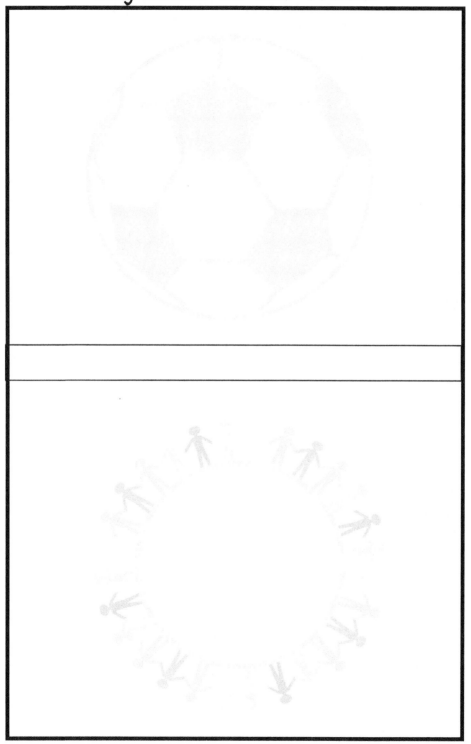

Date

- - - - - -

Weather

The Opponent Team

Match Time

Match Location

Feelings Toward The Match

Highlight Of The Match: ---------------

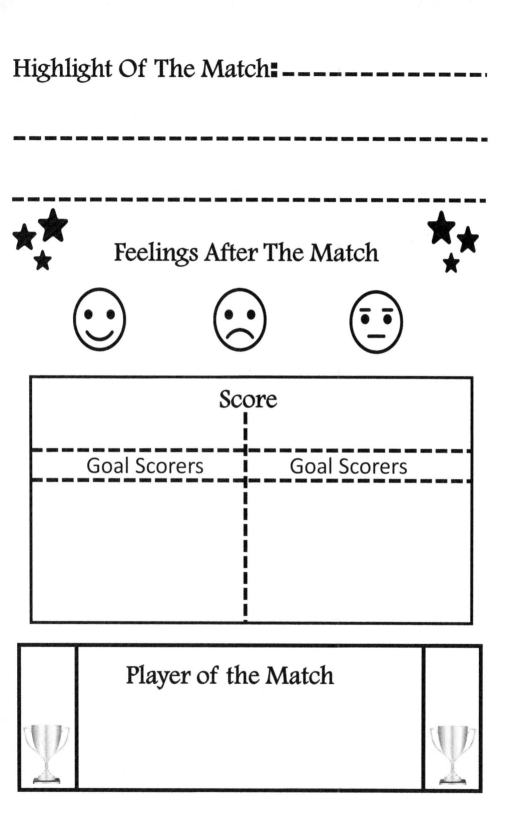

Feelings After The Match

Score

Goal Scorers	Goal Scorers

Player of the Match

Skills To Work On

Tactics for my Next Game

Word of Advice

My Hero of the Week

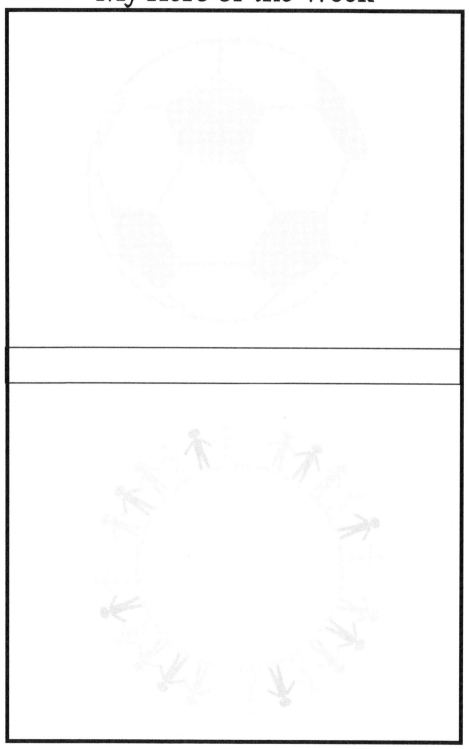

Date

- - - - - - -

Weather

The Opponent Team

Match Time

Match Location

Feelings Toward The Match

Highlight Of The Match: ---------------

Feelings After The Match

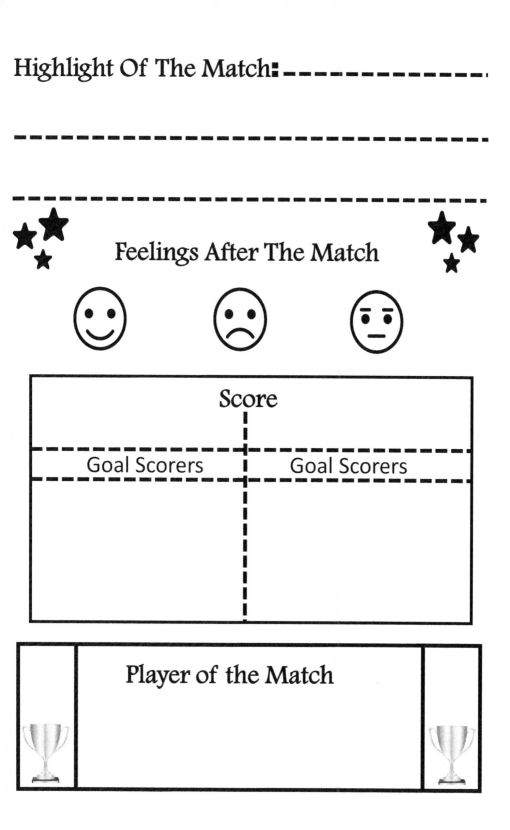

Score	
Goal Scorers	Goal Scorers

Player of the Match

Skills To Work On

_____

_____

_____

_____

_____

Tactics for my Next Game

_____

_____

_____

_____

_____

Word of Advice

My Hero of the Week

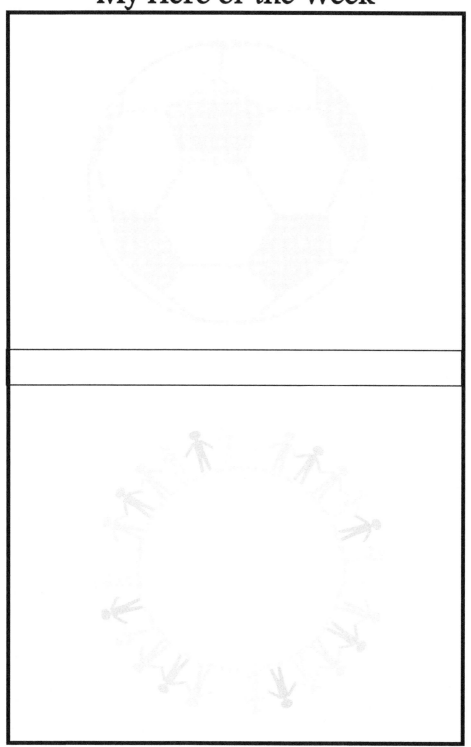

Date

- - - - - -

Weather

The Opponent Team

Match Time

Match Location

Feelings Toward The Match

Highlight Of The Match: ---------------

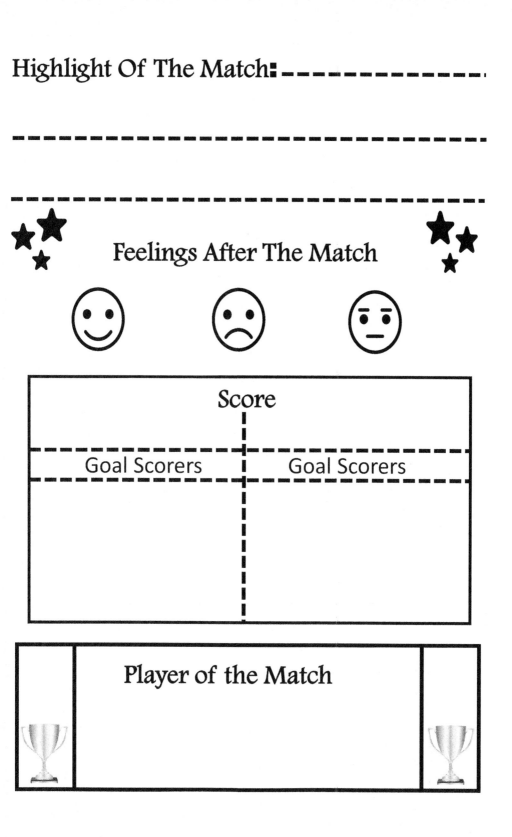

Feelings After The Match

Score	
Goal Scorers	Goal Scorers

Player of the Match

Skills To Work On

_____

_____

_____

_____

_____

Tactics for my Next Game

_____

_____

_____

_____

Word of Advice

My Hero of the Week

Date

Weather

The Opponent Team

Match Time

Match Location

Feelings Toward The Match

Highlight Of The Match: ------------

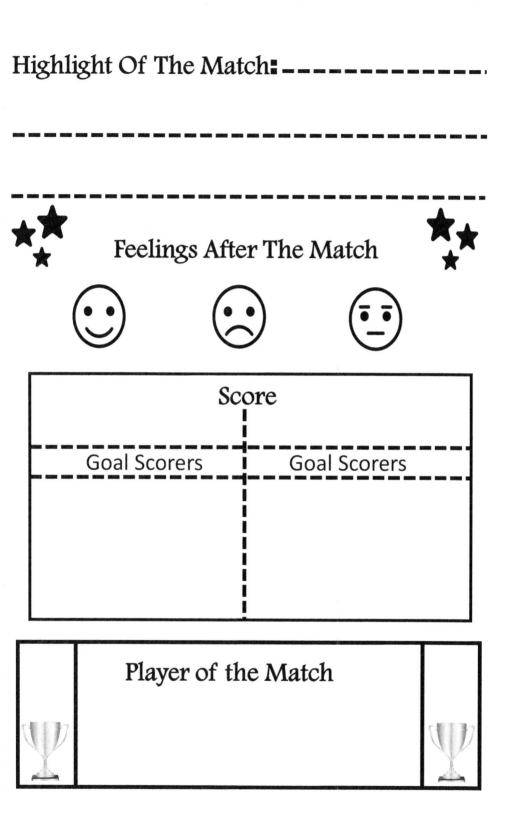

Feelings After The Match

Score

| Goal Scorers | Goal Scorers |

Player of the Match

Skills To Work On

_____

_____

_____

_____

_____

Tactics for my Next Game

_____

_____

_____

_____

Word of Advice

My Hero of the Week

Date

Weather

The Opponent Team

Match Time

Match Location

Feelings Toward The Match

Highlight Of The Match: -- -- -- -- -- -- -- -- --

-- -- -- -- -- -- -- -- -- -- -- -- -- -- -- -- -- -- --

-- -- -- -- -- -- -- -- -- -- -- -- -- -- -- -- -- -- --

Feelings After The Match

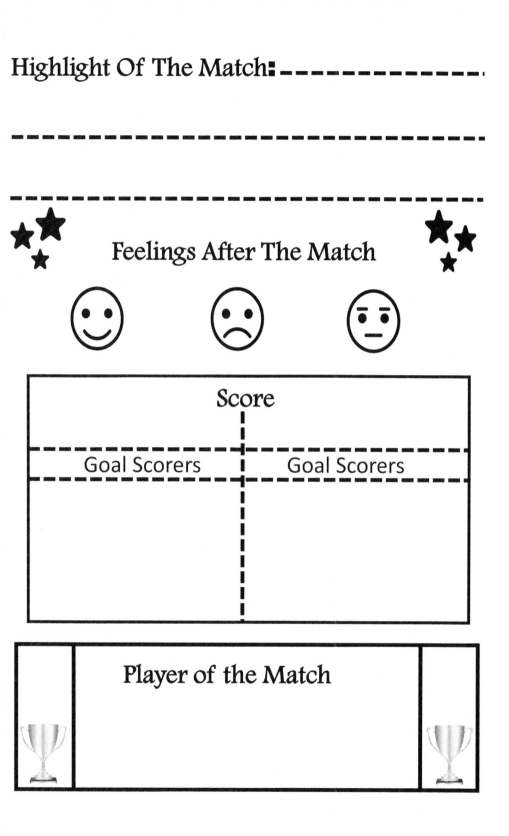

Score

Goal Scorers	Goal Scorers

Player of the Match

Skills To Work On

_____

_____

_____

_____

_____

Tactics for my Next Game

_____

_____

_____

_____

_____

Word of Advice

My Hero of the Week

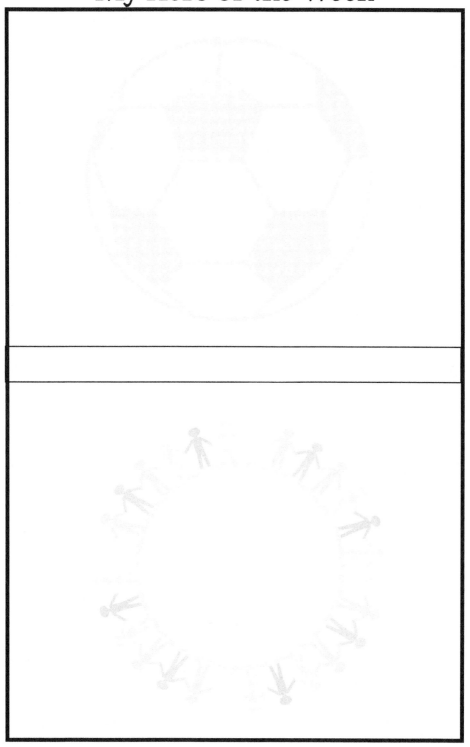

Date

Weather

The Opponent Team

Match Time

Match Location

Feelings Toward The Match

Highlight Of The Match: -----------------

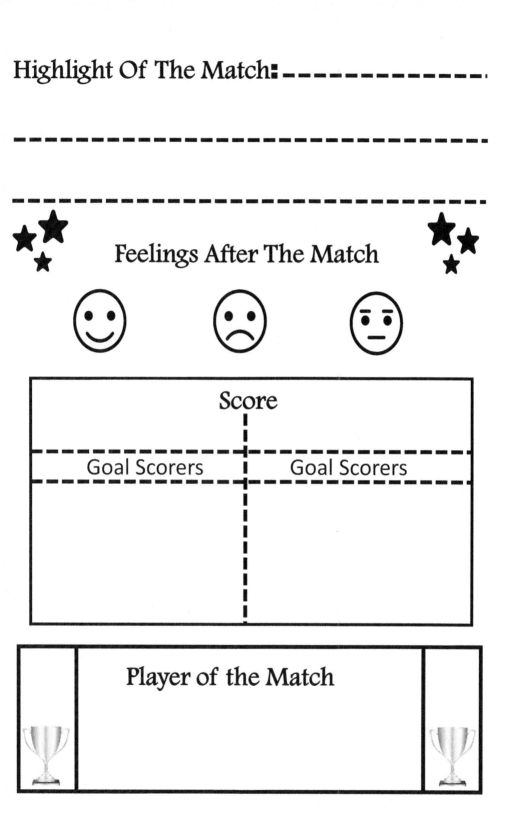

Feelings After The Match

Score	
Goal Scorers	Goal Scorers

Player of the Match

Skills To Work On

Tactics for my Next Game

Word of Advice

My Hero of the Week

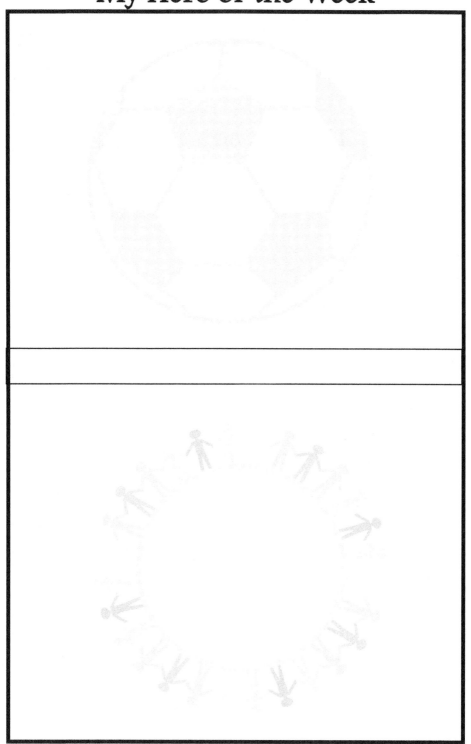

Date

Weather

The Opponent Team

Match Time

Match Location

Feelings Toward The Match

Highlight Of The Match: --------------- ·

Feelings After The Match

Score

Goal Scorers | Goal Scorers

Player of the Match

Skills To Work On

_____

_____

_____

_____

_____

Tactics for my Next Game

_____

_____

_____

_____

_____

Word of Advice

My Hero of the Week

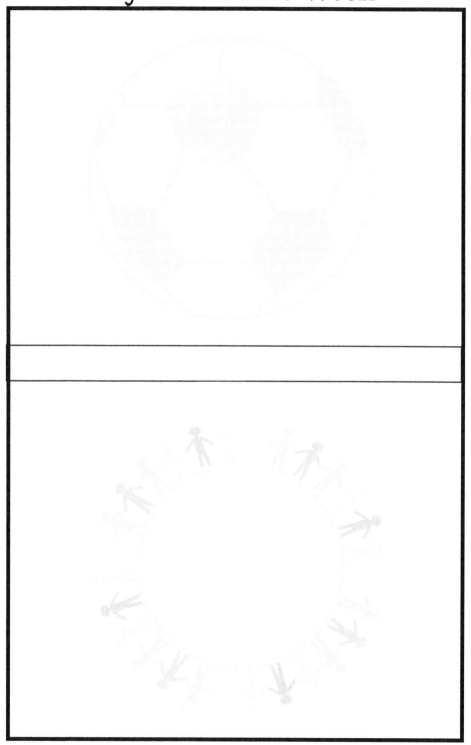

Date

Weather

The Opponent Team

Match Time

Match Location

Feelings Toward The Match

Highlight Of The Match: ---------------

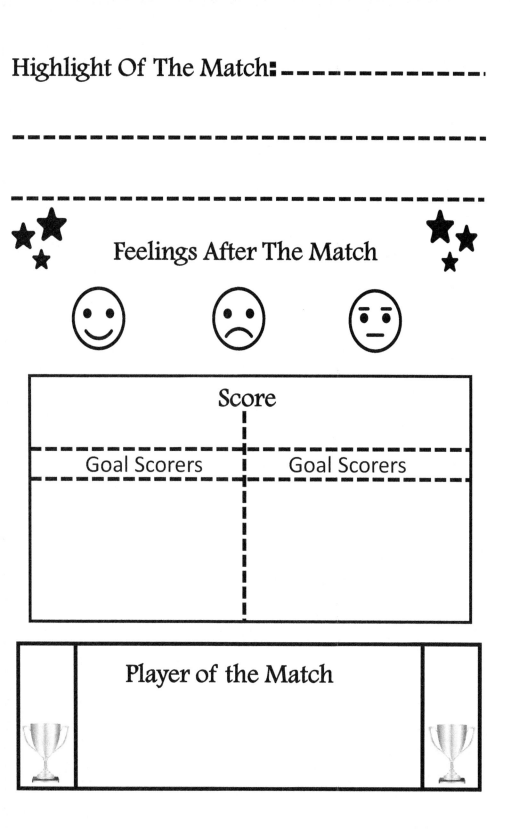

Feelings After The Match

Score	
Goal Scorers	Goal Scorers

Player of the Match

Skills To Work On

_____

_____

_____

_____

_____

Tactics for my Next Game

_____

_____

_____

_____

Word of Advice

My Hero of the Week

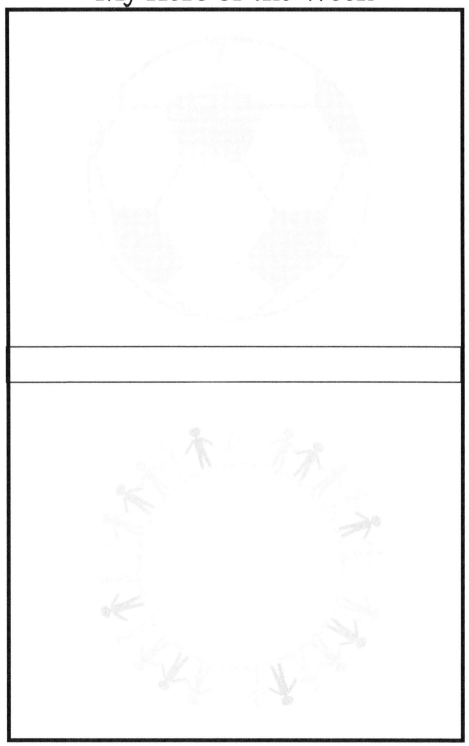

Date

Weather

The Opponent Team

Match Time

Match Location

Feelings Toward The Match

Highlight Of The Match: ---------------

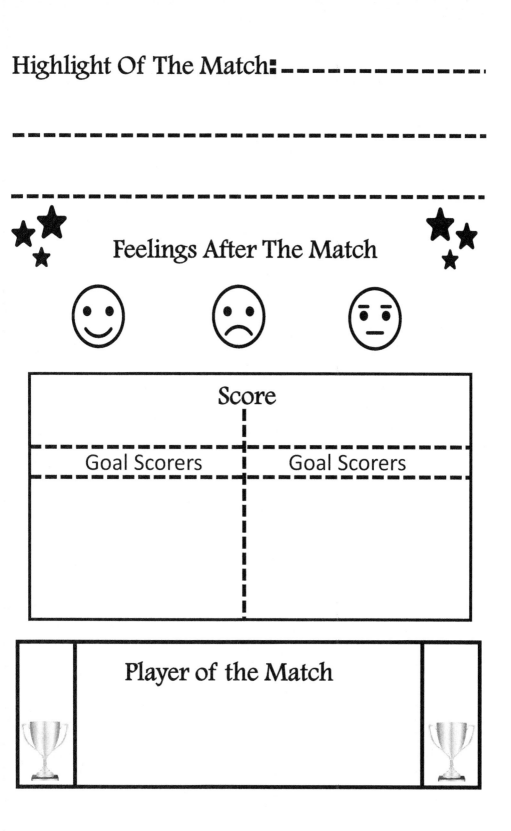

Feelings After The Match

Score

| Goal Scorers | Goal Scorers |

Player of the Match

Skills To Work On

Tactics for my Next Game

Word of Advice

My Hero of the Week

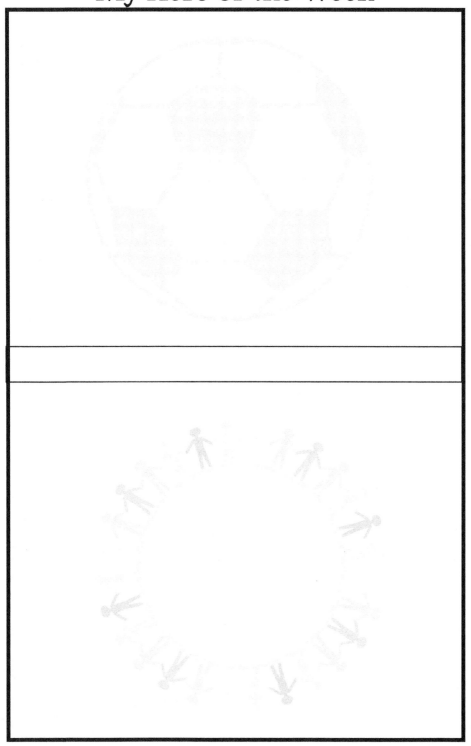

Date

Weather

The Opponent Team

Match Time

Match Location

Feelings Toward The Match

Highlight Of The Match: -------------------

Feelings After The Match

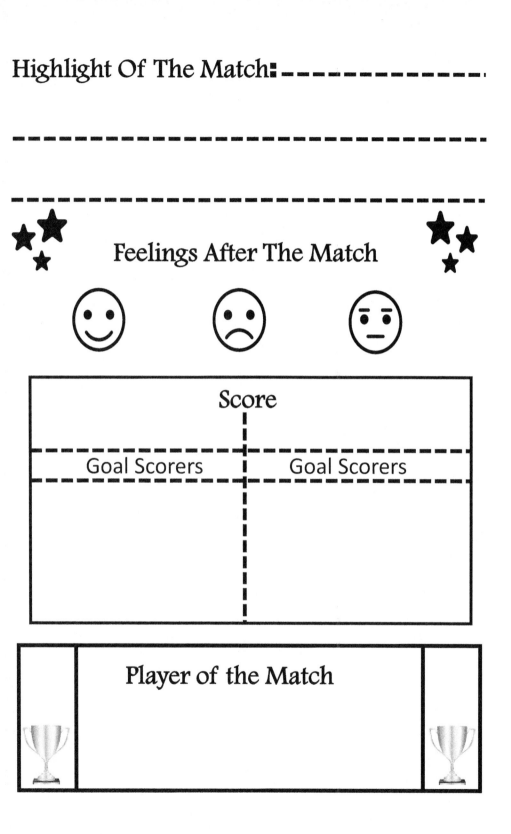

Score	
Goal Scorers	Goal Scorers

Player of the Match

Skills To Work On

_____

_____

_____

_____

_____

Tactics for my Next Game

_____

_____

_____

_____

_____

Word of Advice

My Hero of the Week

Date

- - - - - -

Weather

The Opponent Team

Match Time

Match Location

Feelings Toward The Match

Highlight Of The Match: -------------------

Feelings After The Match

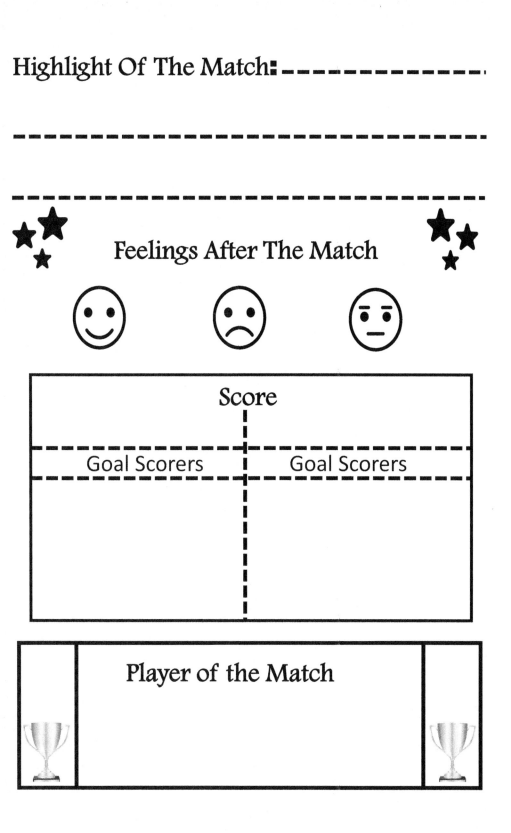

Score

Goal Scorers	Goal Scorers

Player of the Match

Skills To Work On

Tactics for my Next Game

Word of Advice

My Hero of the Week

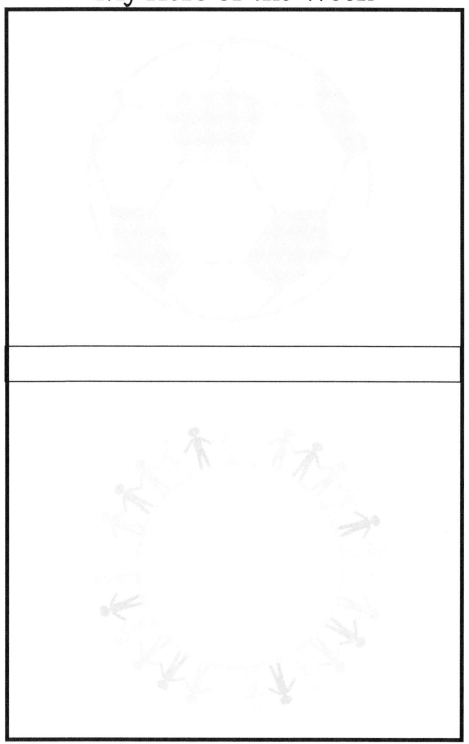

Date

- - - - - - -

Weather

The Opponent Team

Match Time

Match Location

Feelings Toward The Match

Highlight Of The Match: ---------------

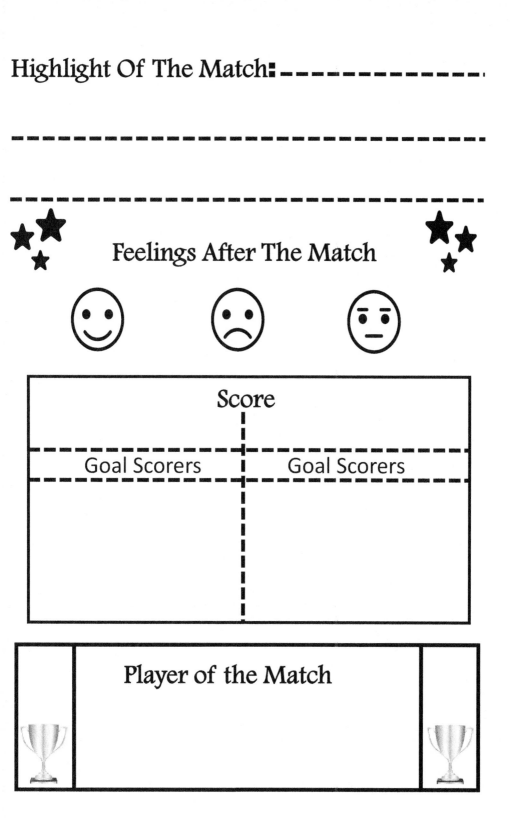

Feelings After The Match

Score

Goal Scorers | Goal Scorers

Player of the Match

Skills To Work On

_____

_____

_____

_____

_____

Tactics for my Next Game

_____

_____

_____

_____

_____

Word of Advice

My Hero of the Week

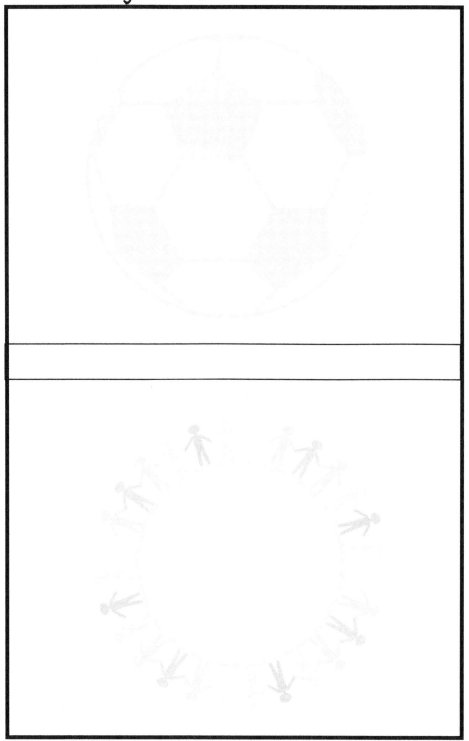

Date

 Weather

The Opponent Team

Match Time

Match Location

Feelings Toward The Match

Highlight Of The Match: ---------------------

Feelings After The Match

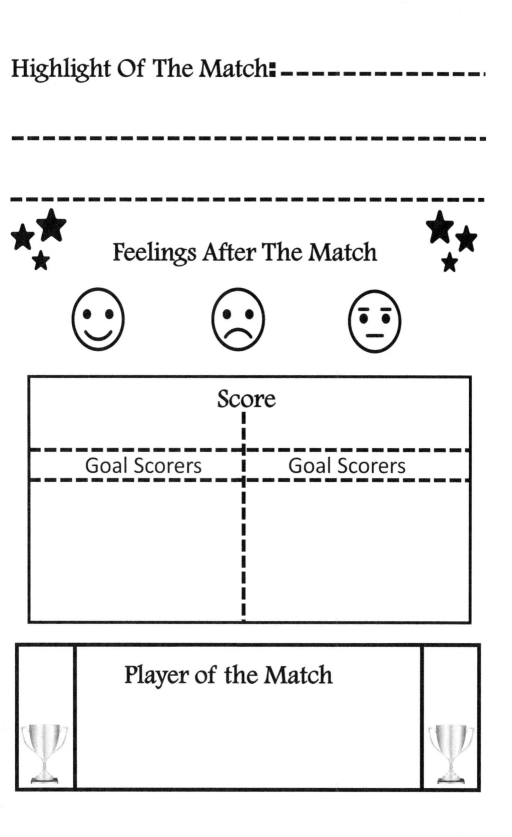

Score	
Goal Scorers	Goal Scorers

Player of the Match

Skills To Work On

_____

_____

_____

_____

_____

Tactics for my Next Game

_____

_____

_____

_____

_____

Word of Advice

My Hero of the Week

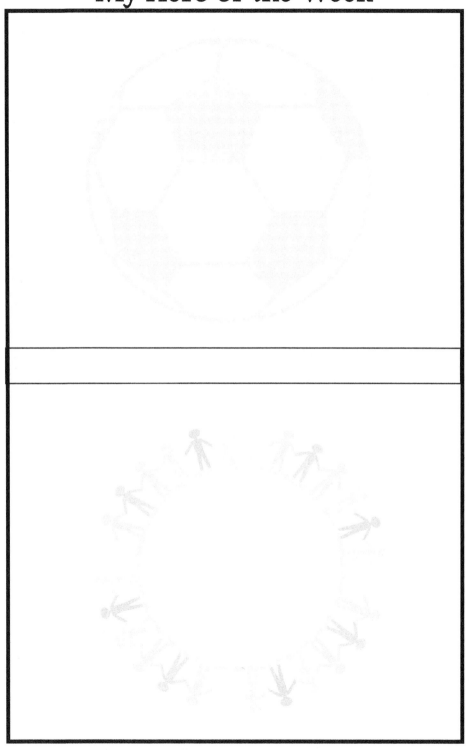

Date

Weather

The Opponent Team

Match Time

Match Location

Feelings Toward The Match

Highlight Of The Match: ------------

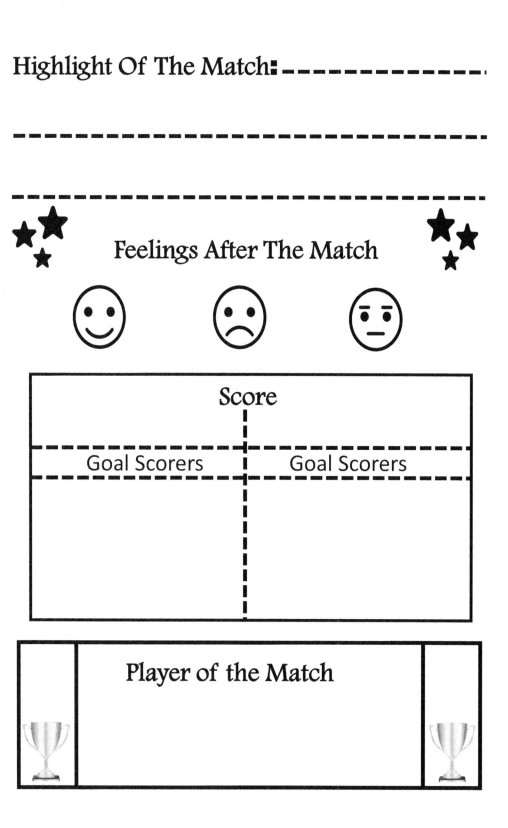

Feelings After The Match

Score

| Goal Scorers | Goal Scorers |

Player of the Match

Skills To Work On

_____

_____

_____

_____

_____

Tactics for my Next Game

_____

_____

_____

_____

Word of Advice

My Hero of the Week

Date

Weather

The Opponent Team

Match Time

Match Location

Feelings Toward The Match

Highlight Of The Match: -----------------

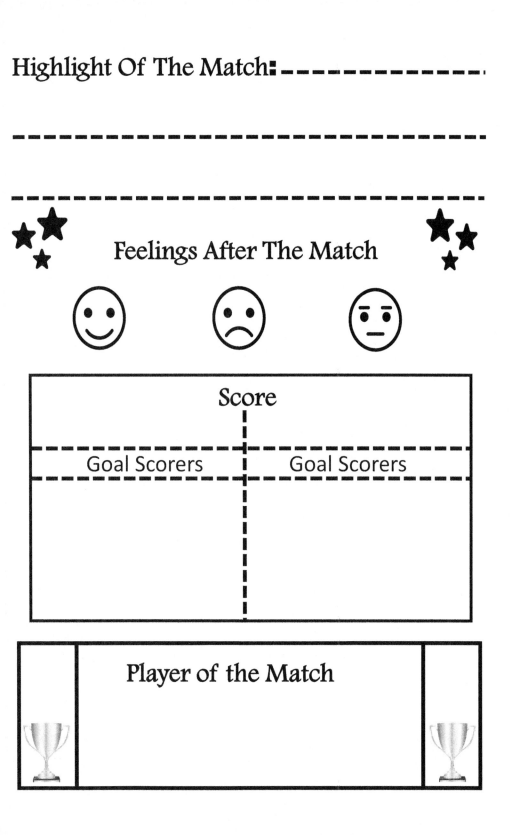

Feelings After The Match

Score

Goal Scorers	Goal Scorers

Player of the Match

Skills To Work On

_____

_____

_____

_____

_____

Tactics for my Next Game

_____

_____

_____

_____

Word of Advice

My Hero of the Week

Date

- - - - - -

Weather

The Opponent Team

Match Time

Match Location

Feelings Toward The Match

Highlight Of The Match: ----------------

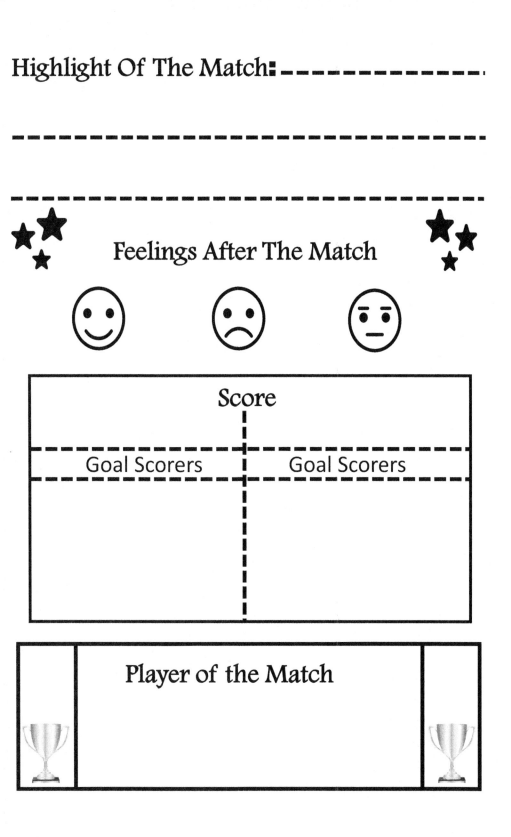

Feelings After The Match

Score	
Goal Scorers	Goal Scorers

Player of the Match

Skills To Work On

_____

_____

_____

_____

_____

Tactics for my Next Game

_____

_____

_____

_____

Word of Advice

My Hero of the Week

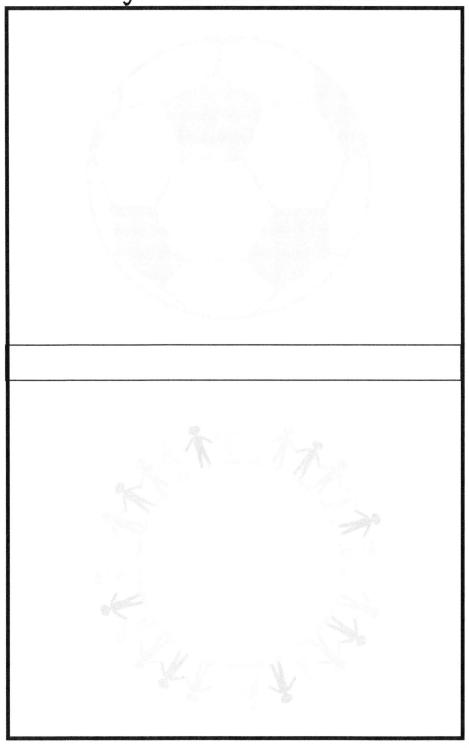

Date

- - - - - -

Weather

The Opponent Team

Match Time

Match Location

Feelings Toward The Match

Highlight Of The Match: ------------ ----- ------------ -

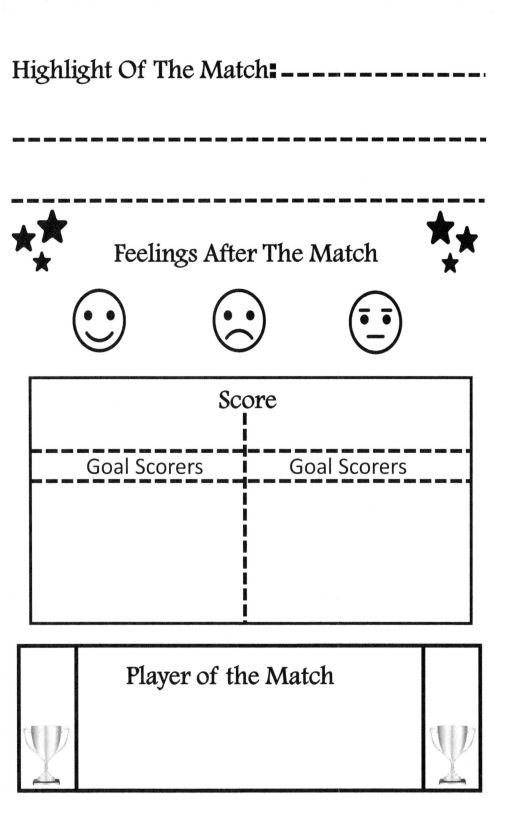

Feelings After The Match

Score

Goal Scorers	Goal Scorers

Player of the Match

Skills To Work On

Tactics for my Next Game

Word of Advice

My Hero of the Week

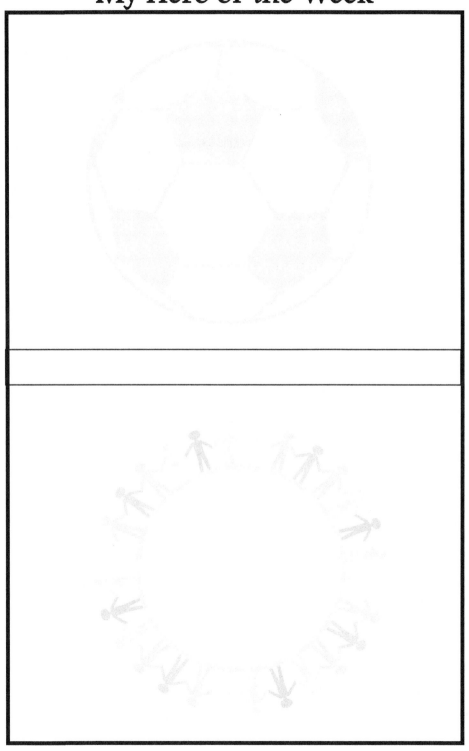

Date

- - - - - -

Weather

The Opponent Team

Match Time

Match Location

Feelings Toward The Match

Highlight Of The Match: ----------------

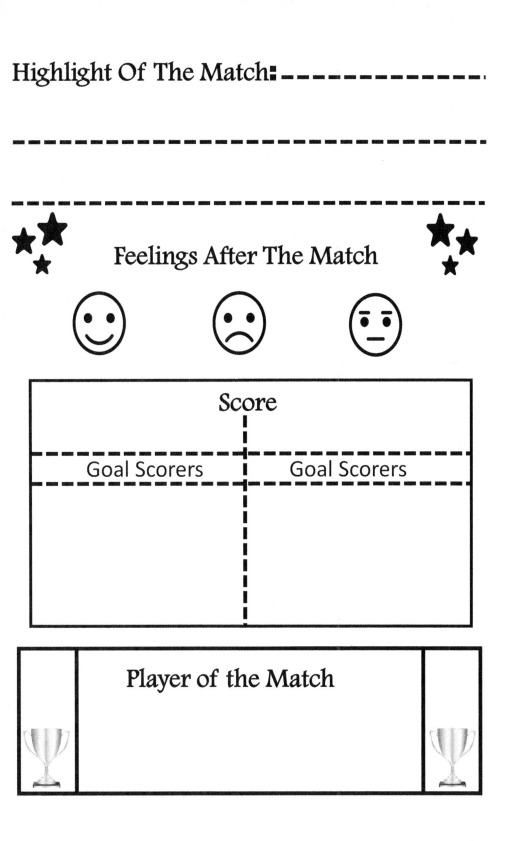

Feelings After The Match

Score	
Goal Scorers	Goal Scorers

Player of the Match

Skills To Work On

Tactics for my Next Game

Word of Advice

My Hero of the Week

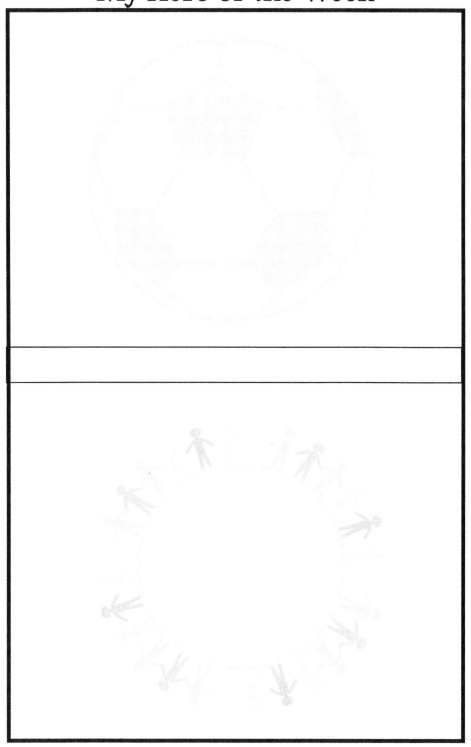

Date

- - - - - -

Weather

The Opponent Team

Match Time

Match Location

Feelings Toward The Match

Highlight Of The Match: ------------

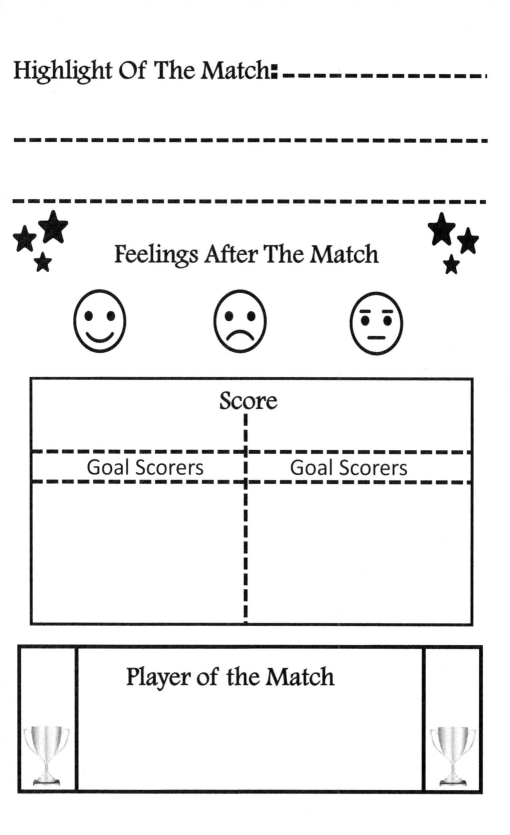

Feelings After The Match

Score

Goal Scorers	Goal Scorers

Player of the Match

Skills To Work On

_____

_____

_____

_____

_____

Tactics for my Next Game

_____

_____

_____

_____

Word of Advice

My Hero of the Week

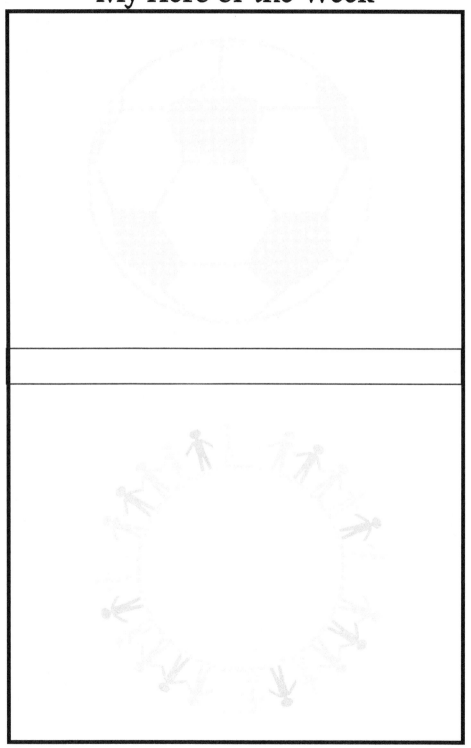

Date

Weather

The Opponent Team

Match Time

Match Location

Feelings Toward The Match

Highlight Of The Match: ---------------

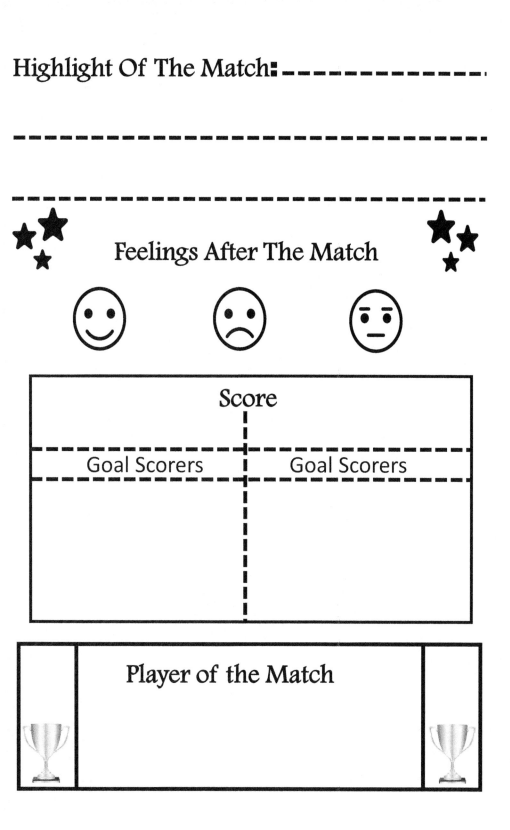

Feelings After The Match

Score	
Goal Scorers	Goal Scorers

Player of the Match

Skills To Work On

Tactics for my Next Game

Word of Advice

My Hero of the Week

Date

- - - - - -

Weather

The Opponent Team

Match Time

Match Location

Feelings Toward The Match

Highlight Of The Match: ----------------

Feelings After The Match

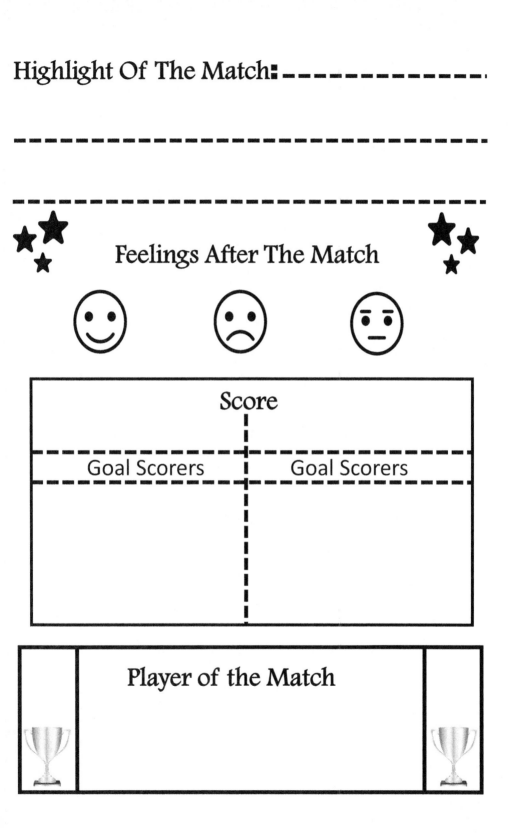

Score	
Goal Scorers	Goal Scorers

Player of the Match

Skills To Work On

_____
_____
_____
_____
_____

Tactics for my Next Game

_____
_____
_____
_____
_____

Word of Advice

My Hero of the Week

Date

Weather

The Opponent Team

Match Time

Match Location

Feelings Toward The Match

Highlight Of The Match: ----------

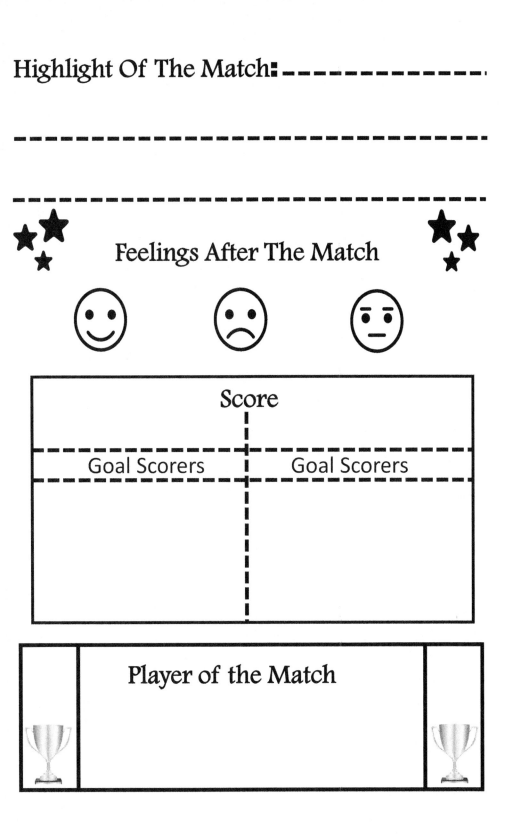

Feelings After The Match

Score

Goal Scorers | Goal Scorers

Player of the Match

Skills To Work On

_____

_____

_____

_____

_____

Tactics for my Next Game

_____

_____

_____

_____

Word of Advice

My Hero of the Week

Date

— — — — — —

Weather

The Opponent Team

Match Time

Match Location

Feelings Toward The Match

Highlight Of The Match: ─ ─ ─ ─ ─ ─ ─ ─ ─ ─

─ ─ ─ ─ ─ ─ ─ ─ ─ ─ ─ ─ ─ ─ ─ ─ ─

─ ─ ─ ─ ─ ─ ─ ─ ─ ─ ─ ─ ─ ─ ─ ─

Feelings After The Match

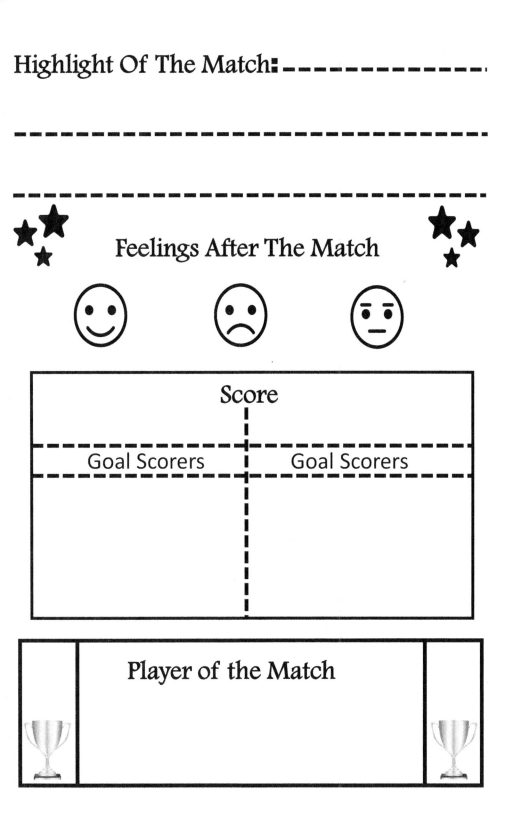

Score	
Goal Scorers	Goal Scorers

Player of the Match

Skills To Work On

_____

_____

_____

_____

_____

Tactics for my Next Game

_____

_____

_____

_____

Word of Advice

My Hero of the Week

Date

Weather

The Opponent Team

Match Time

Match Location

Feelings Toward The Match

Highlight Of The Match: ------------------------

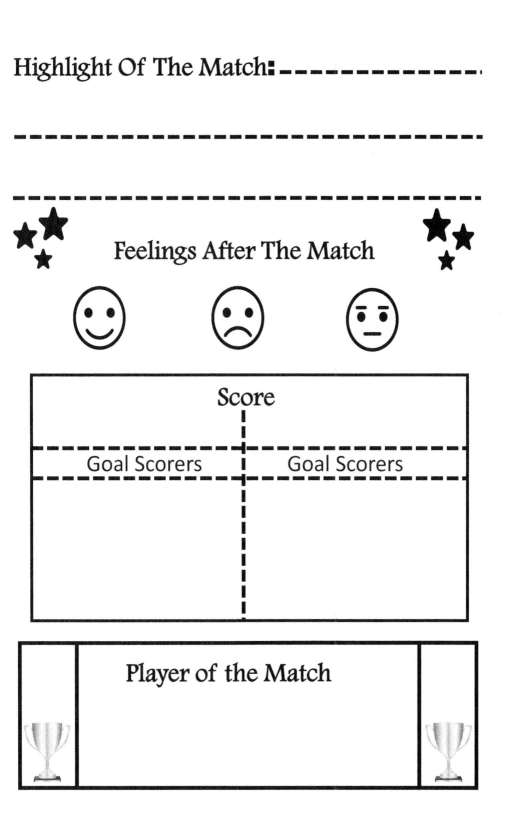

Feelings After The Match

Score

Goal Scorers | Goal Scorers

Player of the Match

Skills To Work On

Tactics for my Next Game

Word of Advice

My Hero of the Week

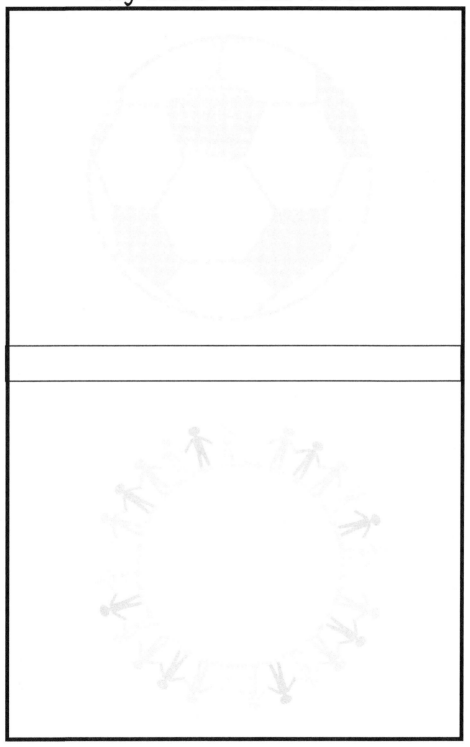

Date

- - - - - -

Weather

The Opponent Team

Match Time

Match Location

Feelings Toward The Match

Highlight Of The Match: ━━━━━━━━━━━━

━━━━━━━━━━━━━━━━━━━━━━━━

━━━━━━━━━━━━━━━━━━━━━━━━

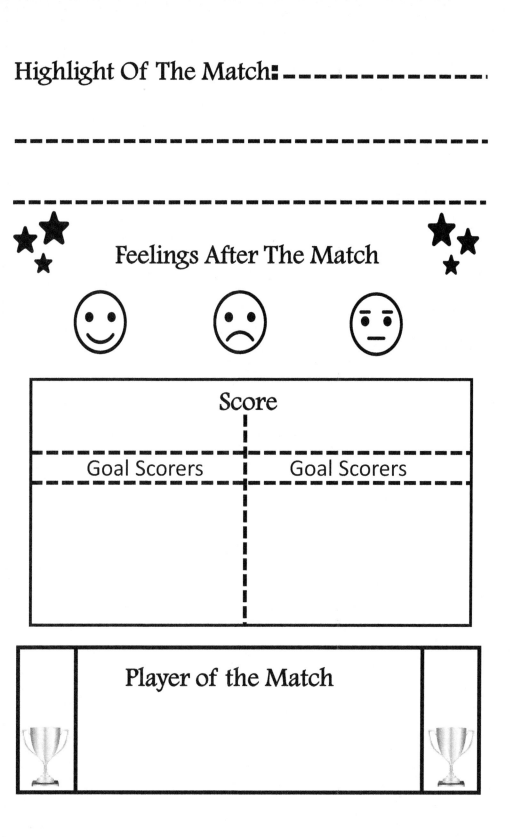

Feelings After The Match

Score

Goal Scorers	Goal Scorers

Player of the Match

Skills To Work On

Tactics for my Next Game

Word of Advice

My Hero of the Week

Date

– – – – – – –

Weather

The Opponent Team

Match Time

Match Location

Feelings Toward The Match

Highlight Of The Match: ----------------------

Feelings After The Match

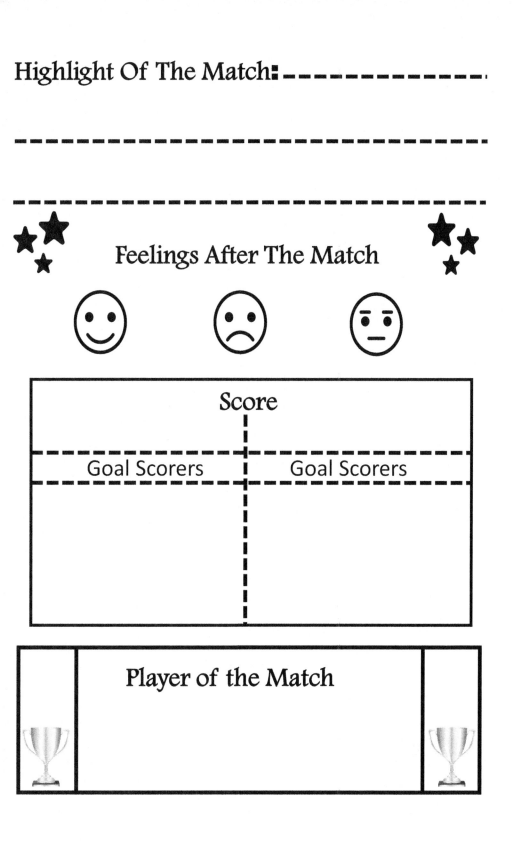

Score

Goal Scorers	Goal Scorers

Player of the Match

Skills To Work On

_____

_____

_____

_____

_____

Tactics for my Next Game

_____

_____

_____

_____

_____

Word of Advice

My Hero of the Week

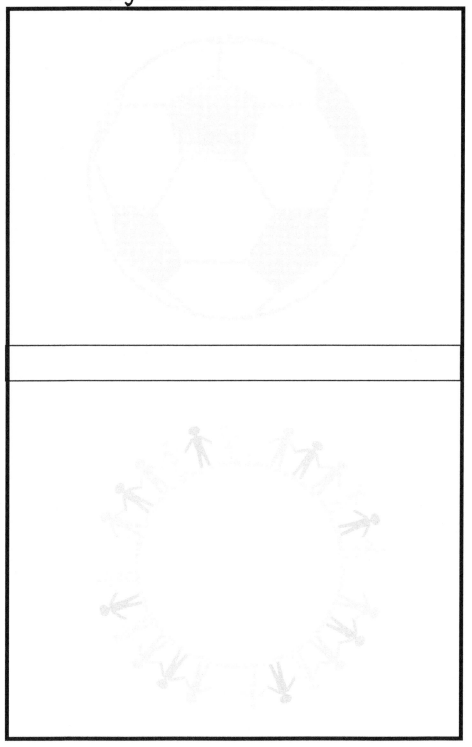

Date

- - - - - - -

Weather

The Opponent Team

Match Time

Match Location

Feelings Toward The Match

Highlight Of The Match: ----------------

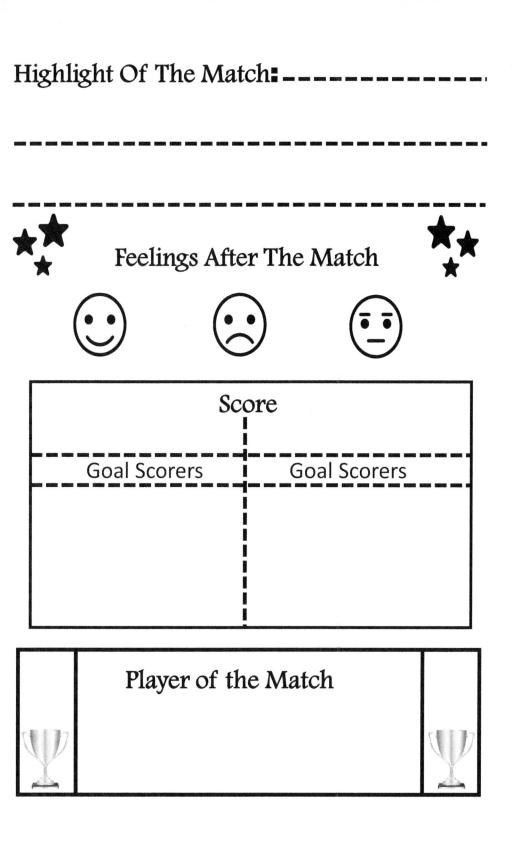

Feelings After The Match

Score

Goal Scorers | Goal Scorers

Player of the Match

Skills To Work On

_____

_____

_____

_____

_____

Tactics for my Next Game

_____

_____

_____

_____

_____

Word of Advice

My Hero of the Week

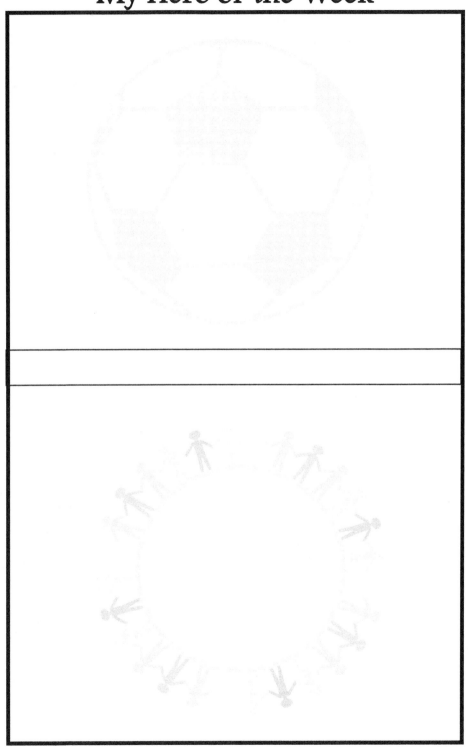

Important Information

Date	Events

Important Information

Date	Events

Printed in Great Britain
by Amazon